**Collins**

# The Trouble with
# Jack

Anne C;

# 1 Dead and gone

The trouble with Jack was that he didn't listen to anyone.

He didn't even listen to me, his girlfriend.

That's why I was standing on Hutton Moor holding a bunch of flowers. There was a small card attached to them that said, *Miss You, Jodie XXXX.* I had tears in my eyes.

One of Jack's friends, Steve, was beside me. Jack's brother, Micky, was sitting in his car, waiting for us in the car park.

"I can't believe he's been dead a whole year," I said.

"A year," Steve said.

That wasn't quite true. It was a year, two days and fourteen hours since I'd last seen him.

It was raining hard, so I put my hood up. The raindrops were hitting the paper around the flowers. Steve was getting wet. He didn't seem to notice the weather. Maybe he was thinking about Jack, I thought.

"The trouble with Jack was that he thought he knew best," Steve said.

I nodded. "Don't go on the moor by yourself," everyone told him. His friends, his brother and me. We all said it over and over.

Jack had a habit of doing what he wanted.

A year ago, after school, he'd gone out on the moor on his bike. It had been at the end of September, and he'd wanted to cycle part of the coastal route. I saw him at school, and he told me he'd come round to my house about nine. I waited for him but he didn't come.

I never saw him again.

Steve was moving around as though he was ready to go. I wasn't sure why he had come in the first place. I hadn't asked him. He'd just turned up.

"Where shall we put the flowers?" he said.

I looked round. All I could see was miles and miles of moorland, grass and bushes and heather. It was huge. That was why Jack got lost on it. His body was never found, so there was no headstone or grave. There was nowhere to leave flowers.

"You could put them over there," Steve said.

He pointed to a bench on the edge of the visitor's car park. It was old, and one of the armrests had broken off. I nodded. Jack and I had had a habit of sitting there. Sometimes we would sit there for ages after dark, and kiss. It was a good place.

I placed the flowers on it. I knew they'd die in a couple of days, but that didn't matter.

"Ready to go?" I said.

Steve nodded. We headed back to the car. Micky was standing by it, with an angry look on his face. He was in a bad mood. Since Jack had disappeared, Micky was always in a bad mood. He held the car door open and I got in. Steve shook his head and said he wanted to walk. I didn't try and change his mind.

As we drove away, I looked out of the back window of the car. The rain was covering the glass, making it difficult for me to see. Somewhere on that moor, I thought, was Jack's body. I hoped he was covered up. I didn't like to think of him lying out in the wet and cold.

# 2 Coffee and tears

Later that day I met up with some of Jack's friends at a café in town. There were four of us: me, Steve, Jordan and Alex. We'd got together to talk about Jack. We were sitting next to the window. Outside, it was still raining hard. People were running past the café with their hoods up or holding umbrellas.

"Do you remember when Jack decided to build his own bike?" Jordan said.

"How long did it take him?" Alex asked.

"Three months," I said.

For three months Jack had used his brother's garage to build it from scratch. He'd found the frame of an old bike in a skip. He'd cleaned it up and then bought some wheels from a car boot sale. His brother, Micky, had found the other parts online.

I often sat in the messy garage and watched them put it together. When I was bored, I spent time looking at Micky's noticeboard, which was covered in layers of posters, photos and notes. Once I offered to tidy it up and get rid of out-of-date stuff, but Micky told me to leave it alone.

In the middle of it, pinned on top of other things, had been a poster for the Viper Cycle Race. This was the race that Jack had been keen to win. Everyone wanted to win the Viper Race.

"I don't know why he didn't just buy a new bike. Everyone else did."

"He wanted to see if he could do it," I replied.

I understood this side of Jack. I liked to make jewellery. I could buy a necklace in a shop for a couple of pounds, but I liked to make my own. That way no one else would ever wear the same as me.

"It was a challenge," I added.

"Like riding the moors on his own?" Jordan said.

We all sat quietly holding our drinks.
I remembered Jack when he'd first gone onto
the moors on his home-made bike. He'd been
wearing the cycling jacket that Micky had bought
for him. It was a bright orange colour with navy
stripes down the sleeve. Jack loved it. He'd sewn
some blue lettering onto the back. It said, COBRA.
That was his racing name, COBRA, like the snake,
deadly. There was no other jacket like it, he'd
said. Just like his home-made bike. One of a kind.
Just like my jewellery.

I'd given him a belt bag as a present. He'd put
his mobile phone in it so that he didn't lose it. And
a puncture repair kit. *Thanks so much!* he'd said,
giving me a hug.

"I have to go," said Steve.

"I should be getting off as well," Alex said.
"See you later, Jodie."

After they left, Jordan looked like he had something to say.

"You know that ringtone Jack used?"

"The howling wolf?" I said.

"Where did he get that?"

"He downloaded it."

It was a sad howling sound. It made me shiver but Jack loved it. Whenever he couldn't find his phone, he got me to ring his number and then we'd hear the howling. It was as if there was a wolf in the house with us.

"The odd thing is," Jordan said, "I heard it a few days ago. I was playing footie at the sports centre. We had the floodlights on because it was dark. It was about half seven and it was near the end of the game. Then I heard it. This wolf howling."

"How odd. I never heard anyone else with it."

"It sounded exactly the same. Exactly, howl for howl."

"Did you see whose phone it was?"

Jordan shook his head.

"It was coming from the trees on the edge of the football pitch, like it really was a wolf. I guess some kids were probably hanging round there. It actually spooked me out a bit. What with it coming up to the first anniversary."

"It's just a ringtone. Maybe Jack got it because he heard someone else's."

"Maybe," Jordan said.

He was worried, his forehead creased. Soon after that we left the café, and he went his way and I went mine.

# 3 Thinking of happy days

It was getting dark as I walked home. When I got there, Mum was ready to go to work at the local college, with her files and laptop on the table.

"There's some pasta for tea. Just heat it up in the microwave. How did it go today? Up on the moor?"

"It was good. I'm glad I went. We left some flowers. Steve turned up!"

"Did he?"

"I was surprised. He's been a bit distant ever since …"

"I know. A death hits people in different ways."

I didn't answer. Hearing the word *death* always made me feel gloomy.

"I'm glad you're moving on from it, Jodie. It's time to leave it behind."

"I'll never forget Jack."

"I know."

We were silent for a minute.

"Listen, the college autumn fête is in a couple of weeks," Mum said. Why not set up a jewellery stall? You said you would. You've got boxes of the stuff in your room."

My mum was right. My room was full of necklaces, bracelets and earrings that I'd made over the last year. I'd told her that I was going to start a small business, but since Jack went missing I hadn't had the heart.

"Maybe," I said.

Later that evening I got out my phone and looked through my photographs. I had about fifty of me and Jack in various places. We'd only been together for three months before he disappeared, but we'd had a habit of spending a lot of time together.

My favourite photo was the one that his brother Micky had taken of us at the beginning of the 10k bike ride across the moors. It was a yearly race that sixth-formers from a number of schools took part in. Jack was standing by his bike.

He was wearing his orange jacket with navy stripes. The rules said he had to wear a cycling helmet. He hated it though and said it made him look like an alien. I was standing next to him. We were both smiling at some joke Micky had made.

It made me feel so sad.

I put my phone down and lay back on the settee. I put the TV on but after a while I felt tired. I pressed the mute button and watched the pictures until I felt my eyelids get heavy.

I must have drifted off to sleep.

Something made me wake up with a jump. I sat up feeling dazed, still half asleep. I heard it again. An unhappy sound. It was a howl. A wolf's howl.

It was the ringtone of Jack's phone.

For a second I felt afraid. My hands were tense, my fingers stiff.

Then I put my phone down and stood up and forced a smile as if to laugh it off. The sound came from outside in the street, I was sure. I went out to the front door and opened it.

There it was again. The sound of a wolf crying. It was moving away from me, getting lower.

Someone had the same ringtone as Jack had had. So what? Jordan had already mentioned it that afternoon. It was nothing to be upset about.

I closed the front door and went inside.

# 4 Bikes, bikes and more bikes

The following Sunday I decided to go and watch the end of the Viper Cycle Race. Steve and Jordan were taking part. The race took place every year and finished at the sports centre next to our school. It was a tough race, 20k. Jack had planned to go on it, but he'd gone missing a few days before.

I met Alex half way there. As we walked along, I told him about hearing Jack's old ringtone and how Jordan had heard it as well.

"It's really odd that you should say that," he said. "I heard it myself early this morning. I was doing my paper round. It was dark and I was just finishing up, delivering at the last house, when I heard the same thing, the sound of a wolf howling."

He paused. "It made me jump but then this car started up and drove away, so I thought it was probably the driver's."

"Jack was the only one who had it though."

"He can't have been. Other people will have it too, Jodie. Remember how much people liked hearing it. Someone will have found out how to download it."

"How come we never heard it till now? A year after he went missing?"

"Maybe we just never *noticed* it till now."

I nodded. Maybe he was right.

We walked on towards the sports centre. At the front entrance there were groups of kids hanging around, some on skateboards. I headed for the playing fields at the back of the building. It was only two in the afternoon but the sky looked grey and heavy, as if night were on its way.

The finishing line was marked out with banners and coloured balloons. A big crowd was waiting for the first riders to come in off the moors.

I saw Micky. He came over.

"First rider's due in about ten minutes," he said. "Steve might be in the first twenty. Jordan's further behind."

Last year none of the boys raced. They were too worried about Jack.

After Jack went missing, a lot of us went onto the moors looking for him. Every day we went from first light and stayed out until it got dark. There were over a hundred people searching at first.

As the days went on, more and more people dropped out. The police continued, but they took small areas, day by day. They did it slowly, so we all began to realise that they no longer thought they would find Jack alive.

They never found him.

Just then there was the sound of raised voices. People started to move towards the finishing line. I felt myself being carried along.

"Leader's in sight!" Micky said.

People started to clap and call out. It was noisy, with a real feeling of excitement. I watched Micky walk towards the finishing line and wondered whether he was feeling sad about Jack not being here for the race.

Alex had moved a little away from me. We were both swept up by the surge of people heading for the finishing line. I couldn't quite see because most of the people round me were taller. I went on tiptoes but then I just gave up. The winner had come in. I could hear a loud cheer. I would have to find out later. I dropped back to the edge of the crowd and waited for Alex.

Then I saw something which made me look twice. Someone was wearing a cycling jacket that was exactly the same as the one that Jack had owned. It was bright orange with a line of navy down each sleeve.

I was dismayed by the sight of it. Of course there would be others around. It was bought from a cycling website. Jack wouldn't have been the only one to wear it.

The young man who was wearing it looked a little like Jack. He had short cropped black hair and was tall. He looked at me for a moment then he turned away.

That's when I got the shock.

On the back of his jacket was the word COBRA.

Those were the letters that Jack had sewn onto the back of his jacket. That's what made *his* jacket one of a kind.

"I thought I'd lost you."

I turned round. Alex was standing there. The crowd had broken up. There were cyclists coming over the finishing line, one after the other, a small crowd clapping politely for each one.

"You look like you've seen a ghost!" Alex said.

"No, I'm okay." I suddenly didn't want to tell him.

"Jordan's due in any minute. You want to see?"

I nodded. He went off, and I looked over to where I'd seen the boy in the jacket moments before. He wasn't there. I looked around at the different groups of young people standing about, but I couldn't see the jacket or the boy anywhere. Some of the cyclists were wheeling their bikes through the crowd. I saw Micky talking to Steve. Micky was bending down looking at one of the wheels on Steve's bike.

But the boy in the COBRA jacket was nowhere to be seen.

# 5 Alex's surprise

I was still thinking about seeing the boy the next day. I was in the library and I went onto the internet and found the website that sold the jackets. They were still on sale, so there was no reason why someone else shouldn't buy one.

But to put the word COBRA on the back was strange.

I was thinking hard about it when I felt a tap on my shoulder. I turned round. Alex was standing behind me. He was looking worried.

"What's up?" I said.

"Come and have a look at my bike."

"Why?"

"Just come and see."

I logged off the computer and followed him out of the library.

We got to the bike park and Alex wove in and out of the dozens of bikes that were there. Alex's bike was padlocked to a bike rack at the very edge. Alex stood by it with an unhappy look on his face.

"What?" I said, looking at his bike.

He pointed to something that was hanging from the handlebars. A bag of some sort.

"Look at this," he said.

He unhooked the bag. It took me a minute to work out what it was. Then I gasped. It was the belt bag I had bought for Jack. He'd used it for his phone mostly. I put my hand out and took it off him. It was empty but looked scuffed, as if it had been used a lot.

"Why is this here?"

"I don't know. I was passing here just after break. I checked my bike like I always do and saw this. Someone has put it here."

I unzipped the two compartments. There was nothing inside.

"This, plus hearing the ringtone all over the place! Something funny is going on," I said. "Are you going to see Steve and Jordan?"

Alex nodded.

"Tell them we should meet up in the common room after school."

# 6 Talking it through

I was in the common room at four. Steve turned up first. He looked moody, as if he didn't want to be there. Jordan and Alex came together.

"What's up?" Steve said, his mobile in his hand as if he was waiting for an important phone call.

"Odd things have been happening," I said. "Things to do with Jack."

Then I explained about the ringtone and the belt bag. Alex and Jordan backed me up. I also told them all about seeing the boy in the cycling jacket. Alex and Jordan looked shocked.

Steve had no expression on his face.

I waited for a few moments wondering whether Steve might say, *Oh I heard that ringtone too!* or *Something odd happened to me as well!*

But he didn't say anything.

"Has anything funny happened to you?" I said.

Steve frowned and shook his head. I was puzzled by the frown. It looked like he was acting. All he had to do was say *No.*

"These things are probably just coincidences. It's because Jack's been dead a year, and we're all thinking about him."

"That's what I said at first. But what about the belt bag?" Alex said.

"It probably belongs to someone else who uses that bike park. It's dropped off their bike and someone's picked it up and put it on yours."

Now I was frowning. It *could* have happened like that ...

"What about the jacket with the word COBRA on it?" I said.

"COBRA is a famous snake. It's the Viper Race. It would be odd if there wasn't some kind of COBRA there. I'm sure Jack wasn't the first to use it. Look, I have to go. I've got some assignments to finish."

We watched as he walked out of the common room. He'd made us all feel a bit silly.

"Maybe he's right. We're all on edge because it's a year since Jack went missing."

"Yeah, maybe," I said.

# 7 Brother and friend

Later that night I was restless, so I went out for a walk. It was dark and cold, and I could smell fireworks in the air. I was thinking about what had been said. Maybe Steve was right, I thought, and we were all making too much of small things. I stood at a crossing, shivering and feeling tired and gloomy.

I wondered what I was going to do for the rest of the evening. I had homework, but after that I thought I'd make some earrings. I had some beautiful glass beads that would look great. Maybe I'd also sort out all my other jewellery and think about the fête.

I walked on. I was still troubled by the things that had happened.

I decided to go and talk to Jack's brother, Micky. I walked in the direction of his street, feeling a little nervous about going to see him.

I liked Micky, but since Jack died he'd been a bit distant, as if he didn't want to know me any more. He was twenty-five and had once been married. Now he lived with his parents. He bought and sold motorbikes and cycles, and worked on them in his parents' garage.

In the months that I'd been Jack's girlfriend, he'd been funny and nice. But now I didn't feel so relaxed with him.

He'd loved Jack. He was always hugging him and patting him on the back. Sometimes I'd get to the garage and find them in the middle of a long conversation about football or cricket or the Tour de France.

He often gave Jack a fiver or a tenner to spend for no reason at all. And he helped him build his bike.

When Jack went missing, Micky looked dreadful. Of all of us, he seemed to find it the hardest to accept Jack must be dead. He didn't work for weeks.

I got to his street and thought about what I was going to say.

*Hi Micky! I wanted to talk about Jack.*

*Oh, Micky, I'm glad I've caught you. I just wanted to mention something about Jack.*

*I'm worried, Micky. Some odd things are happening and it's got something to do with Jack.*

The light was on in his garage. I walked round to the side door and heard the sound of people talking inside. The door was open a couple of inches. I pushed it a little bit. The garage was brightly lit up, and Micky was down the other end with someone else. They were both looking at a bike.

I hesitated. Should I just go home? Then Micky turned round and saw me there. The other boy looked up from the bike.

I recognised him straight away. It was the boy from the Viper Race who had been wearing Jack's cycling jacket. Then I saw the jacket itself hanging on a hook on the wall. I could make out the letters C and B from the word COBRA.

"Who's he?" I said. "And why was he wearing that jacket at the Viper Race last week?"

Micky blew through his teeth. The other boy looked awkward.

"This is Harry, a mate of mine. His younger brother goes to your school. They've been helping me out a bit."

"Are you going to tell me what's going on?"

"You'd better come in, Jodie."

# 8  Truth and lies

Harry took his bike and left.

Micky got a chair for me to sit on.

"You remember that day when Jack went missing?" he said.

I did remember it. Of course I did; how could I forget? It was a normal school day, and Jack had said he'd come round to my house about nine.

"Everyone thought that he'd gone out for that ride alone," Micky said.

I nodded.

"But I know he didn't."

"How?"

"That afternoon we had a terrible row. I was mad at him for a load of reasons. Mainly the way he used to ignore people's advice. He loved cycling. He thought he knew it all. Like the helmet I bought him to wear. He kept saying he would wear it, but hardly ever did."

"I know."

"Bad things were said. He told me to mind my own business. He said I was too interested in his life and I should get a life of my own."

I'd heard some of this story before in the days after Jack went missing. It was one of the reasons Micky found it so hard to deal with Jack's disappearance.

"I told him to get lost. I told him not to ask me to fix his bike any more or take him to races. Then he left, and I didn't see him again. At the time, when he went missing, I thought he must have hated me."

"Micky, you have to let this go. You have to move on with your life." I sounded like my mum. Hadn't she been saying those very things to me?

"The thing is, Jodie, I was wrong. A couple of weeks ago I was looking for a flier for something. I was sure I'd pinned it onto my noticeboard."

I looked at Micky's noticeboard. It was crammed full with posters and tickets and photos. It looked heavy, as if it might suddenly fall off the wall.

"I found this."

He held a piece of paper out. I took it. It was a note in Jack's handwriting. It gave me a shock to see it.

*Micky, sorry about the row! You're right – I'll take more care on the bike. I'm doing the coastal path with a mate tonight. But one thing – I'm definitely not wearing the helmet! PS Lost my phone again. See if you can find it in the garage, Jack*

**BMX
MOUNTAIN BIKE**

**PEAK
RIDERS**

about the row!
, I'll take more
bike.
e coastal path
tonight.
g, I'm definitely
the helmet!

PS Lost my phone again.
See if you can find it in the
garage,
Jack.

It felt funny reading Jack's words written down. It was almost as if I could hear his voice in my ear.

"Where did you find it?"

"It was on the noticeboard. Jack must have come back in here after the row and pinned it there. Then one of my mates pinned a flier for a bike rally over the top of it. I never saw the note. It had been there for almost a year and I never saw it."

I looked over to the noticeboard. In my head I pictured Jack coming into the garage and pinning it there. Maybe he had a last look round for his lost phone before he left.

"So when I found this, I knew for sure that he'd gone out with one of his mates."

"Have you asked them?"

"I asked them all at the time, but they said no. Now I've found Jack's note, I felt I had to put a bit of pressure on them."

I stared at him and thought about the things that had been happening.

"Tell me what's been going on, Jodie," he said.

I told him everything that had happened. I explained about Jack's old ringtone and how me, Jordan and Alex had heard it. I also told him about finding Jack's belt bag on Alex's bike.

"And that's it? Just you, Alex and Jordan noticed these things?"

"Just us," I said. "Steve hasn't seen anything."

I remembered Steve shaking his head and frowning when I asked him about it an hour or so before. At the time I'd thought he was being over-dramatic.

Micky looked as though he was thinking hard.

"I'm going to be straight with you, Jodie. I've been trying to spook them."

"Spook them?"

"Frighten them, confuse them. I took the ringtone off Jack's laptop. Harry carried it round and played it in various places so that you would all hear it. And I got a cycling jacket and I put the letters on the back of it. I bought another belt bag and Harry's brother put it on Alex's bike."

I was dismayed.

"But why involve me?"

"I feel bad about that but I thought if I did it to *you,* then you would get them talking about it."

Micky was right. They were boys. They'd probably never have talked to each other about it.

"The fact that Alex and Jordan told you about what happened to them, confided in you, tells me that they were not with Jack that night."

"And Steve was?"

"Steve must have heard the ringtone. I also got Harry's brother to place one of Jack's football scarves around the handlebars of his bike. I think the fact that he's denying he's heard or seen anything is because he knows what happened to Jack."

I frowned. It was a hard thing to swallow.

"I always wondered if he knew something about Jack's disappearance," Micky said. "He hardly speaks to me. He crosses the street if he sees me. When we were up at the moor on Jack's anniversary, he couldn't look me in the eye. Then, at the Viper Race, he nearly jumped out of his skin when I talked to him. Whenever I see Jordan or Alex, they just act normal."

"What are you going to do?"

"I've got a plan."

Micky smiled. It was the first time I'd seen him smile in a very long time.

# 9 Friend or foe?

I sat in Micky's garage trying to take in the things he'd told me. Had Steve been with Jack on the night he went missing?

"You don't think that Steve *killed* Jack?" I managed to say.

"I don't know. I've tried not to think about it. That's why I've decided to find out, once and for all."

"How?"

"I want you to ring Steve. You're going to tell him that you've heard that the police have found some evidence on the moors relating to Jack's disappearance. I think this will scare him into going to the place where he was last with Jack."

"You mean where Jack's body is?" I said, feeling a little sick.

He nodded.

"This is horrible!"

"I know it is. But I have to know what happened to my brother."

"How will you know when he goes onto the moor?"

"I'm going to use this."

Micky picked up a gadget that looked like a mobile phone. I took it from him and saw that it had a small screen with a map, like a sat nav. The map showed the street where I live and the surrounding streets. There were three red dots on it.

"What is this?"

"It's a GPS tracker. I fixed three tiny transmitters under the bike seats of Jordan, Alex and Steve. I've been waiting for one of them to go onto the moors but apart from the Viper Race, none of them have. Now I know it's Steve, I can turn the other two off."

Micky fiddled with the monitor. When I looked at it again, it just had one red dot on it.

"After you've spoken to him, I expect him to take his bike out and head up to the moors. I can track the route he takes and where he ends up. I'm going to follow him."

"That's if you're right."

He shrugged. "Will you ring him?"

I only thought about it for a second.

"I will, but I want to come with you. You're Jack's brother but I was his girlfriend. I need to know too."

He frowned. But then he nodded.

I got my phone out and made the call. The ringtone sounded but then it went to voicemail. My voice was shaking a little as I left a message.

"Hi, Steve. I've just heard something I thought you'd want to know. The police have found something up on the moor to do with Jack. It seems that they're going to open up the case again. It's brilliant news, because we might finally find out what happened to him. Ring me when you get this message."

Then I ended the call. We both sat there looking at the GPS monitor.

The minutes ticked by. I began to think maybe Micky was wrong. That he'd jumped to the wrong conclusion about Steve.

Then the red dot on the monitor began to flash on and off.

"He's on the move," Micky said.

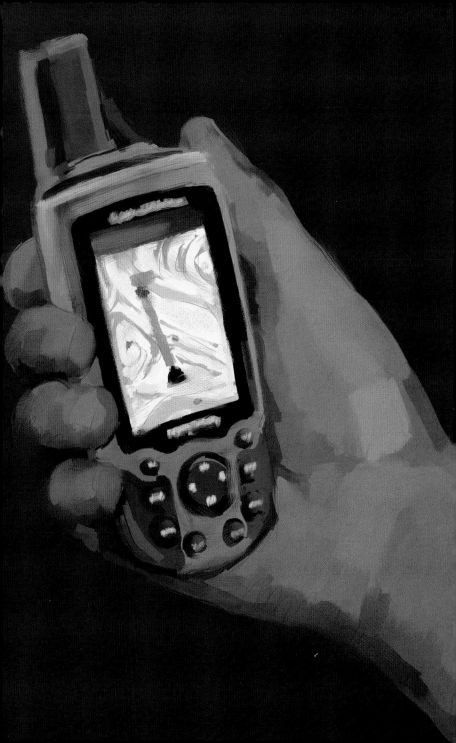

# 10  On the moor

Micky left me on my own in the garage while I rang my mum and told her that I was seeing some of my old girlfriends. He came back a few moments later with two walking jackets. He handed one to me.

"That's Jack's coat," he said. "Here's a small torch. Put it in your pocket. Let's get going."

We drove along the lane that ran alongside the moors and parked in the empty car park. It was windy. I could feel the car move at each gust of wind.

Micky turned on the inside light and we both looked at the monitor. The red dot that was the transmitter was moving slowly north east.

"He's heading up the coastal path. There's a track that runs for about five kilometres alongside the path. It's used by construction workers and moors rangers. We'll drive along it then we'll get out and walk."

"Won't he see us?"

Micky shook his head. "We'll drive without any lights."

I gripped my seat belt. The trip was beginning to feel a bit dangerous.

"You hold the GPS. Use your torch to see it. Tell me if he goes off the coastal path."

The moor was dark, and it seemed as though we were driving into a black hole. As the car went on, slowly I could see some shapes. The sky was a little lighter than the ground. The bushes along the side of the track were grey.

After a few moments I could see the track ahead. It wasn't as dark as I'd first thought it was.

I looked down at the GPS. The red dot was moving along the path. I checked the scale of the map and worked out that Steve was a couple of kilometres ahead of us. I could feel the car shudder in the wind and I wasn't looking forward to getting out and walking.

We drove on in silence. After a while I could see that the red dot was closer to us.

"I think he's about a kilometre away," I said.

"This track turns inland soon. When it does, we'll park and walk."

We parked and got out of the car. I zipped up Jack's old walking coat and pulled the hood up. I wished I had gloves and a scarf with me, but I had to make do with the coat.

"Where's the sea?" I said.

"The sea's about a kilometre away. The coastal path gets closer further north."

"Oh."

"Ready?" Micky shouted above the wind.

I nodded and we began to walk into the darkness. Micky was in front. Even though it was dark, we didn't need the torches. The clouds were beginning to clear a little over in the east, so there was some moonlight, even if we couldn't actually see the moon. I could see the path up ahead as it rose and fell, and then rose again.

It was getting a bit steeper as we went on. All around it was perfectly silent. I wondered where Steve was.

A few moments later, Micky stopped.

"He's up ahead," he whispered. "He's turned off the path and he's heading for that rocky area over there."

I looked hard into the darkness and could just see some movement up ahead. I couldn't make out what it was but I could see some huge slabs of rock that seemed to jut out of the ground.

"Come on, let's speed up."

Micky went faster and I tried to keep up with him. When we got closer to the rocks, I could see a haze of light coming from behind one of them. It was torchlight.

Micky pointed to the rock and we went forward more slowly.

I could hear something: the sound of someone's breathing. We both stood at the edge of the rock and looked around. Steve was there, on his knees, pulling at bits of wood and throwing them away. There were rocks, too, and he was picking them up and throwing them behind him. He seemed frantic, completely absorbed in what he was doing.

He was digging something out of the ground. It gave me a bad feeling. We both watched. It seemed as though we were both paralysed.

Steve kept on digging with his bare hands. He didn't know we were there. I turned away. I couldn't bear to look.

Then I saw Micky take his phone out of his pocket. I had a mad thought. Was he going to ring someone? Text someone?

Instead, I heard the sound of a wolf howling.

It sounded lonely and was loud enough to be heard above the rush of the wind. He was playing Jack's ringtone.

Steve jumped. He made a gasping sound. He stood up shakily, backing rapidly away from the hole he'd been digging.

Micky turned the ringtone off and switched his torch on.

The light lit up the whole area. Behind the giant rocks, I could see the pile of earth and branches that Steve had thrown there.

"What's down there, Steve?" Micky asked.

Steve shook his head. Now he couldn't speak or move. He was like a frightened deer frozen in the headlights of a car.

Micky stepped across to the hole. He looked down and shook his head. He waved me over. I didn't want to go but I took a couple of steps. I almost closed my eyes, I was so afraid of what I might see.

The wind gusted and nearly blew me over, but I held my ground and walked until I was next to Micky, looking down at where Steve had been digging.

"Oh no," I whispered. "You were right."

There, underneath the branches and stones and earth, was Jack's bike.

Steve had buried it.

# 11 A grim find

Steve was sitting on one of the rocks, his head in his hands.

He was crying.

"Where's Jack, Steve? What happened to him?" Micky said.

Steve began to shake his head.

"WHERE IS HE?" Micky shouted.

Steve pointed beyond the rocks.

"Take us there," Micky said.

"It's about ten minutes away," Steve said, his voice shaky from crying.

"You lead, we'll follow."

Steve started to walk. He went off the path onto the moor itself. He had his torch on and we had ours. None of us spoke. We made a strange procession on the moors. Three young people in search of a body. We walked over a flat area and felt the force of the wind like an invisible hand pushing us here and there.

After what seemed like a long time, Steve came to a stop. It seemed as though we were in the middle of a wilderness. We were certainly a fair way off any of the cycling or walking paths. Steve pointed towards a small hillock that was covered in moss and bushes.

"Over there."

We both looked. In my head I had this odd idea that Jack might just be sitting there, waiting for us. *Where've you been?* he might say. But it was crazy. Jack was dead.

"You go first," Micky said.

Steve walked towards the hillock. He climbed upwards until he came to a rock that was flat, like a paving stone. The three of us stood on it.

"Where is he?" Micky said, his voice low and with a hint of anger.

"He fell down there," Steve said, pointing to an area of brambles and bushes ahead of the place where we were standing.

I was puzzled. The hillock wasn't that high and the sides weren't steep. If Jack had fallen, why hadn't someone found his body?

"It's an old shaft or a cave, I'm not sure which."

He fell down a *hole in the ground.*

Steve took a couple of steps forward. He went carefully, as though walking on ice. Then he stopped and pointed towards the ground.

"There."

Micky stepped forward. I followed him.
He shone his torch on the ground. There, between
the thick gorse bushes, was a gaping hole.

"It might be an entrance to some caves, I think."

"How deep is it?" I said.

I'd heard about holes opening up on the moors.
There were always stories of dogs falling down old
mine shafts.

"Jack fell down there? How?"

"I don't know," he said, crying again, wiping
his face with the back of his hand. "We decided
to cycle off track. We were having a kind of race.
It was Jack's idea. I didn't want to do it. It was
dark! Jack was ahead and I was calling to him to
stop. I'd had enough. I just wanted to go back on
the coastal path and go home, but he kept going
further and further. I said it was dangerous but he
never listened. That was the trouble with Jack. He
wouldn't listen to anyone else!"

Steve sobbed, then took a deep breath and carried on. "I was afraid we would get lost or injured. It was bitterly cold but he just kept going. He finally stopped here. I got off my bike and I was furious with him. We had a row, and I pushed him. He stumbled backwards. I went forward to grab his hand and he must have thought I was going to hit him because he edged back, and then he just disappeared. It was so sudden. He didn't even shout out. One minute he was sliding backwards along the ground and the next he was gone!"

"What did you do? Didn't you try and get him out?"

"Course I did! I reached down. I called out. I sat here for ages calling him."

Micky was kneeling by the hole in the ground. I could see that it was partly covered by bracken and gorse bushes. He put his hand into it and felt around. "It feels like a slippage."

"What do you mean?"

"If there's been a lot of water, the caves and underground shafts sometimes fill up. The earth moves. Out here, off the track, it could be months or years before anyone notices it has happened."

He stood up and looked down at it. He swore over and over.

"So Jack fell down a long way? Or into water?" I said.

"I don't know! I can't tell."

He turned to Steve. His face was grave.

"Why didn't you call out the rescue services?"

"I would have. If he'd called out, or if there'd been any sign of life. But it was completely silent. I thought I'd killed him. I was sure I'd killed him."

Steve looked awful. He was shaking and moving about from one foot to the other.

"I panicked," he went on. "I didn't know what to do."

"But you hid his bike."

"Because I thought he was dead! I was scared. I thought someone would blame me."

"If you'd left his bike out, maybe one of the helicopters or rescue services would have seen it. They would have found him."

"I didn't think. I just panicked."

"You were looking after yourself!"

Micky grabbed Steve by his jacket. He pulled him round so that his back was in front of the hole. Then he made him walk backwards.

"Wait!" I said.

I had a horrible feeling Micky was going to do something he would regret. His face was twisted with rage.

"You can't know that for sure!" he shouted. "Jack could have been knocked out down there. He could have been unconscious. Maybe he came round after you left. Maybe he sat down there for days waiting to be rescued."

"I didn't mean it to happen." Steve was sobbing.

"But it did, Steve, and it's your fault!"

Micky gave him a shove. He did it at an angle though, so Steve fell away from the hole that Jack had fallen into. Micky walked off. I followed him. I could hear Steve calling from behind me but I couldn't bear to look at him again.

# 12 Flowers again

They recovered Jack's body the next day.

The rescue service brought it down from the moor on a stretcher. A post-mortem showed he had died from drowning. The cave opening must have been full of water. Micky said it was a relief to know that he hadn't suffered too much.

The police spoke to Steve many times. We heard that he spent hours in interviews going over his statement. In the end, he wasn't charged with anything. It was an accident, they said, and nothing Steve could have done would have saved Jack. Steve had to live with his conscience.

No one spoke to Steve. He went to stay with his dad who lived in Durham. None of us knew if he was ever going to come back.

Jack's funeral was a sad day. It seemed like the whole school was there. I stood in the cemetery as they lowered his coffin into the ground. Beyond the cemetery was the moor. I looked at it and realised that Jack had been buried on it for over a year. Now he was being buried again.

If only he hadn't been so headstrong. If only he hadn't gone on the moor at night. If only he had listened to Steve and not gone riding off track.

But the real trouble with Jack was that he was dead, and we would miss him all over again.

After the funeral, Micky and I went out onto the moor to the place where Jack fell down the hole. I put some flowers there and next to them I placed a necklace made from my favourite glass beads.

Micky laid down the orange jacket with the word COBRA on the back. Underneath he had sewn some new letters: *Rest In Peace.*

# Reader challenge

## Word hunt

**1** On page 43, find a verb that means "packed".

**2** On page 61, find an adjective that means "distressed" or "crazy".

**3** On page 72, find an adjective that means "serious".

## Story sense

**4** Why had Jack decided to build his own bike? (pages 7–10)

**5** How do you think Jodie felt when she was at the cycle race? (pages 20–27)

**6** What things did Micky do to try and frighten the others?

**7** What did Jodie think when Micky told her he thought Steve was involved with Jack's death? (pages 48–54)

**8** Why do you think Steve decided not to tell the rescue services about Jack? (pages 72–74)

William Collins's dream of knowledge for all began with the publication of his first book in 1819. A self-educated mill worker, he not only enriched millions of lives, but also founded a flourishing publishing house. Today, staying true to this spirit, Collins books are packed with inspiration, innovation and practical expertise. They place you at the centre of a world of possibility and give you exactly what you need to explore it.

Collins. Freedom to teach.

Published by Collins Education
An imprint of HarperCollins*Publishers*
77-85 Fulham Palace Road
Hammersmith
London
W6 8JB

Browse the complete Collins Education catalogue at **www.collins.co.uk**

Series consultants: Alan Gibbons and Natalie Packer

10 9 8 7 6 5 4 3 2 1
ISBN 978-0-00-754621-3

British Library Cataloguing in Publication Data.
A catalogue record for this publication is available from the British Library.

Commissioned by Catherine Martin
Edited by Sue Chapple
Project-managed by Lucy Hobbs and Caroline Green
Illustration management by Tim Satterthwaite
Proofread by Hugh Hillyard-Parker
Typeset by Jouve India, Ltd
Production by Emma Roberts
Printed and bound in China by South China Printing Co.
Cover design by Paul Manning

## Acknowledgements

The publishers would like to thank the students and teachers of the following schools for their help in trialling the *Read On* series:

Southfields Academy, London
St Mary's College, Hull
Queensbury School, Queensbury, Bradford
Westergate Community School, Chichester

# Your views

**9** Did you suspect Steve was hiding something? What were the clues in the text?

**10** If you were Micky, would you have reacted to Steve in the same way towards the end of the story? Give reasons.

## Spell it

With a partner, look at these words and then cover them up.

- home-made
- twenty-five
- sixth-formers
- post-mortem

Take it in turns for one of you to read the words aloud. The other person has to try and spell each word. Check your answers, then swap over.

## Try it

With a partner, act out the scene between Jodie and Micky in the garage (pages 41–54). Think carefully about the body language and voice you use.